DIARY OF A NINJA KID

"An Alien Invasion; Aliens v Ninjas"

- BOOK 3 -

(A Funny Adventure for Kids: Ages 6 -12)

Written By
C A Treanor & I Dosanjh

Illustrated By
Bex Sutton & Nazifa Tasnim

purposes only. All effort has been executed to present accurate, up to date, reliable, complete information. No warranties of any kind are declared or implied. Readers acknowledge that the author is not engaged in the rendering of legal, financial, medical or professional advice. The content within this book has been derived from various sources. Please consult a licensed professional before attempting any techniques outlined in this book.

By reading this document, the reader agrees that under no circumstances is the author responsible for any losses, direct or indirect, that are incurred as a result of the use of the information contained within this document, including, but not limited to, errors, omissions, or inaccuracies.

DEDICATED TO

For my beautiful kids, who support me and helped
me bring my stories to life.

AUTHOR NOTE

We would like to thank you, our readers,
for joining us on Michael, Larry and Rocky's
adventure!

For the opportunity to receive lots of
exciting extras and to keep up to date with our
next books, please subscribe to our mailing list
through our website, carolinetreanorintbooks.
com/subscribe, and like our Facebook page, @
CATPublishingInternational.

TABLE OF CONTENTS

BOOK DESCRIPTION

As you may know by now, my name is Michael Carter and I am a ninja.

Yes, I am only 12 years old and yes, I am a real ninja. If I had a penny for every time people have asked me that when I tell them this story, I would be able to afford my own spaceship!.

Speaking of spaceships, what is in the giant one that landed at the airport? Did the aliens bring whole families to Earth? It is our job to find out.

With my grumpy sister in tow, me and my fart brother, ninja dog, and three very normal friends set out to investigate the very suspicious spacecraft.

Will what we find inside save the Earth? And what will happen when a very suspicious voice starts talking to us over a radio?

Seems like there is an even bigger adventure to come.

DEAR DIARY

More and more zombies started appearing around the world. They seem to be stronger, faster and stinkier. But even though they are more dangerous now, they are no longer our only threat. The stupid aliens have been landing ship after ship at the airport. Larry and I have been monitoring them very closely. We have been watching their every move. The alien population on our planet has drastically increased and we need to do something about it. Together.

Eve has been managing the new survivors at the campus and my parents have been a real help too. I'm happy we found them. Who knew that parents could be so cool? And they are actually ninjas too? What?

I'm still a little on the fence about Madison. She is still awful, and I contemplate throwing her to the zombies at least twice a day.

I don't think I'm ready to get along with her just yet. She has to make a big personality change if we are going to work together without me feeding her to the zombies. And boy, do we need to work together. There is no way for a single person to survive in the wild anymore. Teamwork is just as useful as a master blaster.

We have one mission: Get rid of the zombies so we can focus all of our energy on the aliens. We can't fight two enemies at once. But maybe, just maybe we can beat them if we take them on separately

Wish us luck!

CHAPTER 1: WAKE UP!

I watched as Larry approached Madison's bed. He didn't make a sound. His footfalls were silent, as if he was walking on air. All of the people on campus were already going about their duties. All except one…

Madison was still in bed, sleeping while everyone else was hard at work. Needless to say, this made some people angry. Some people meaning Larry. As a true fart brother, Larry instantly hated Madison when he met her. He said she was spoiled and bratty, which honestly, I couldn't have said it better myself.

Larry has made it his life's mission to make Madison's life as miserable as she's made mine over the years. This was why Larry was my best friend in the whole world. He had my back and he was willing to do anything for me. Just like I was willing to do anything for me.

My fart brother looked over his shoulder, as if sensing me watching him and put his index finger over his mouth, motioning for me to stay quiet. I mimicked zipping my mouth shut. I could tell that Larry was up to something. He was definitely giddier than he usually was. I didn't know if that excited me or made me nervous. Whatever Larry was going to do, I knew that it was going to be hilarious.

I watched as he snuck closer to her bed, tiptoeing around the other beds in the cafeteria. It was getting a little crowded. We were going to have to think about where to put all of the other people if more survivors showed up. Larry was having a tough time snaking his way through the beds to get to Madison's, but he didn't give up. Oh now, this was going to be good. The only time Larry was this focused was when he had a master plan in the works.

When Larry finally reached Madison's bed, my stomach twisted. I knew exactly what he was about to do. I did it to him once before and it seemed like it was a bad enough experience to do it to Madison too. Larry positioned himself in front of her open, drooling mouth. She was slightly snoring too. Not for long, I thought. Not for long.

Larry picked up one leg and let it rip. The sound echoed through the cafeteria.

Madison gasped and sat up. That was the wrong thing to do. She breathed in the smell of Larry's fart and choked, gagging when the smell hit her. She yelled something about being able to taste it. I could just imagine how horrible that must have been. It was bad enough smelling Larry's farts, never mind tasting them!

I doubled over laughing as Madison screeched like a banshee. Larry ran toward me, afraid that Madison might whack him if she got her hands on him. Honestly, if she did, he deserved it.

Madison was still spitting in the background when Larry finally reached me, grinning so wide it split his face in two.

"That was amazing," I said in between laughing fits. Every time my sister said something about the smell or gagged, it brought on another fit of laughter.

"What can I say, kid?" Larry put his hands on his hips and pushed his chest out as if he was a superhero. In his ninja suit, he really did look like one. "All I can say is that you are very, very much welcome."

"You are a true fart brother," I said and in unison, we both lifted out right legs and farted. Madison was still yelling at us as we left the cafeteria, leaving her with our butt stench.

CHAPTER 2: TRICK BALL

I watched Rocky run after the ball I pretended to throw, trying to figure out why it was so easy to trick him even though he was still a ninja dog. It was strange and something I was probably never going to understand. When Rocky reached a certain point on the football field fenced in along with the rest of the campus, he turned around, sniffed the air and started running back toward me. I was wondering how long it was going to take him to figure out that there was no ball for him to fetch.

I didn't hear Larry until he cleared his throat. I let out a small, nervous fart as he startled me. It was one of those that didn't really smell like anything. I might as well have sneezed or coughed. Still, the squeak made me smile and Larry nodded in approval. "Only a real fart brother can let out such a magnificent sound by accident."

I smiled proudly, but Rocky demanded my attention as soon as he got back, scratching at my hand closed around the ball. This time I really did throw it and Rocky zoomed over the field, catching it midair. If there were any doubts of him being a ninja dog, they were gone now. No normal dog could ever jump that high to catch the ball. Rocky had to be a very special dog to do it. I smiled. I was so lucky to have him.

"You know, we could train him to do more than just fetch balls," Larry said.

I looked over at him. "What do you mean?"

"I mean that there are many, many things that he can do that we don't even know about. It's inside of him. We just have to figure out how to bring it out."

"Do you think he knows about all those skills?"

Larry nodded. "Of course. He knows how to do all of that. I don't think it's training him as much as training ourselves. We need to be worthy of his awesomeness and we have to learn how to command him to do certain things at certain times."

"How do we figure out what he can and can't do?"

Rocky was back now, sniffing my butt before rubbing his behind on my leg to get attention.

Larry shrugged. "We ask him."

"We ask him?" I repeated. I was so confused.

"Like this," Larry said, then turned to Rocky, then said, "Sit, boy." On command, Rocky sat, wagging his tail. "Now, I am going to ask you some questions 'bout your abilities and you are going to answer with a nod or a shake of your head. Do you understand?"

On cue, Rocky nodded, telling us that he understood exactly what Larry was saying.

"Hmm," Larry tapped his chin with his index finger. "Can you jump off buildings and land on your feet?"

A nod. Wow, I didn't know he could do that.

"Let me try," I said before Larry could ask his next question. "Can you shoot laser beams out of your eyes?"

Rocky shook his head. Oh well, it was worth a shot.

Larry chuckled. "How about fart bombs?"

This got a very, very enthusiastic nod. Larry and I looked at each other and grinned. This was useful to know. It might just save our lives in the future.

"Guys!" It was Danny running toward us. Larry and I frowned at each other and when our newest teammate reached us, heaving for breath, he held up a finger to tell us to wait before we asked any questions.

When he finally calmed down and caught his breath, he looked at me and said, "Your parents are back from the patrol and they have news. Eve has called a group meeting in ten minutes. I was sent to fetch the two of you." Rocky growled at him. "Three of you," he said quickly. "I was sent to fetch the three of you."

I wondered what my parents had found.

CHAPTER 3: SHIPS, BIG ONES

"What's going on?" I asked as I approached the crowd of people gathered around my parents. They smelled awful, but that was expected. They came from the outside world after all. They had to blend in with the zombies that were getting stinkier and stinkier by the day.

"We were waiting for you to announce what we saw," my mom said, looking a little too worried for my liking. I didn't like this one bit. Larry and I shared a glance. If ninjas were worried, the rest of the world had to be worried as well. "The aliens have landed."

"But we knew this already," Madison said, crossing her arms. It was so like her to make obvious statements. She didn't even let our parents finish. I glared at her. She deserved the mouth fart more than anyone and I wish Larry's fart had been even more pungent than it was. She deserved it.

Dad nodded. "Yes, but not these ships."

"These ships are huge," Mom interjected. "They can probably carry a thousand aliens all at once."

"How many of those ships have landed?" I asked.

"Only one that we could tell. But there are more coming. I can't think that this is the extent of their race. If they really did want to make Earth their home, they have to bring over their entire planet. Which, unless their entire planet was the size of Texas, is not here yet."

"What do we do now?" Eve asked.

It was Larry who answered. "Michael and I will sneak onto the ship and find out what their cargo was exactly. Perhaps it was weapons instead of people? We won't know if we don't investigate."

"You two can't go alone," Eve argued. "There are too many zombies out there. We can't risk two ninjas that could actually help us. You are too valuable to the campus. You have to take some people with you. I am going too."

Danny huffed a laugh. "This is no job for a girl, Eve. We are friends and everything, but out there is not where you want to be. This calls for big, strong boys."

Eve narrowed her eyes at Danny. "Really? And where are you going to find such a guy? I only see Michael worthy of that title."

Billy chuckled and patted Danny on the back. Eve has never spoken to him, or any of us like that. It was clear that she was serious about going. I was also giggling at the sight.

"After that, it would be a shame not to take Eve with us," said Larry. Eve smiled at him in thanks.

"So Eve, Billy, Danny, Larry, Rocky and I will head to the location the ship landed in. Hopefully we can find something useful. Maybe we can even find some useful weapons that are better against the zombies than the master blasters," I said. Everyone nodded in agreement. Everyone except Madison.

"I'm coming too," she said and most of us cringed. Eve was the only one who kept a straight face but that was only because she was too nice to openly tell Madison that she didn't like her. No one liked Madison.

"You can't come," I said.

Madison raised one eyebrow. "And why not? I am a shinobi too, you know. I have more skills than your friends combined. If the dog can go, so can I."

"He isn't an average dog and—" I looked to Larry for backup, but he only shrugged. As if telling me that I was on my own. I then looked to my parents, who mimicked Larry. I sighed. "Fine, you can come. But I am in charge. You listen to me and Larry. We don't listen to you."

To my surprise, she actually nodded in agreement.

What was my sister up to?

CHAPTER 4: SNOT SANDWICH

When I was younger, my parents told me stories about aliens in space. Of course, I never believed them, but the stories were cool so I went with it. They told stories about aliens and cowboys (which is where the cowboy curtains came from) and their epic battles. Much like our current situation, aliens invaded Earth to take it. I could never understand why anyone would want Earth when there was an entire galaxy out there. There was so much we haven't seen or explored yet. There were so many planets that we didn't even know about. It was all much more exciting than Earth. To me at least. Earth has always been average and boring to me.

Even now, I couldn't understand the alien's fascination with this place.

"Why do you think the aliens came for Earth specifically?" I asked Larry as we sat on the roof of the campus, our legs dangling off the side. We both dug into sandwiches my mother had made for us; no pickles or mayo for me and all the pickles and all the mayo for Larry. His sandwich, needless to say, looked awful.

Larry shrugged as he chewed happily, watching the world beyond the wall around the campus. "Perhaps what we find boring, others find interesting. Think about it," he said. "Are zombies interesting to you anymore?"

"No," I answered truthfully. Honestly, zombies were boring. They were always the same, after the same things. There was nothing different or special about them. They were just zombies.

Larry nodded as if he was expecting that answer.

"Why not?"

I frowned. He should have known why I hate them by now. I answered anyway, humoring him. "Because they're everywhere and they're annoying."

"Exactly," Larry said with a grin. "We are used to them now and instead of being fascinated by them as we used to be when they weren't in the picture, we now hate them."

"So what you are saying is that once things become reality, we hate them?" I asked.

Larry shook his head. "No, not hate. That's a very strong word. No, I'm saying once we have something, we lose interest. We like things we can't have or never think can become a reality. But once the fiction becomes a reality we lose interest and find it boring."

I nodded. He made sense. Perhaps the aliens found Earth interesting because it wasn't something they were used to. Were they going to lose interest as soon as the planet is conquered? That would be a tragedy. All this fighting, all this resistance and tragedy for what? For the aliens to just go back to where they came from? Leaving the Earth barren and void of life?

The thought was depressing.

Larry cleared his throat, then cleared it again. He sniffed and the distinct sound of boogers in his nose made a trembling sound. Larry sighed and closed his one nostril with his finger and blew.

I don't know what Larry was thinking, perhaps he didn't think at all, because as soon as soon as he blew, my sandwich was full of snot.

"Ew!' I said and tossed my sandwich to the side, green slime still trembling from the motion.

Larry laughed. "I'm sorry man, I didn't think it would go that far!" He wanted to give me half of his sandwich but I shook my head. With all that mayo and pickles, I would rather have eaten my snot covered sandwich.

CHAPTER 5: FART CLOUD

The team decided that we would leave the day after tomorrow. With the zombies and aliens roaming about, it was hard to keep track of which day it was. Guessing just confused everyone, so it was easier to take one day at a time and not give it a name.

Larry was lounging in the rec room, one leg over the armrest and one arm over the back. He was chewing on something that didn't smell too safe, but I knew better than to ask what it was. It was better not to acknowledge these things, otherwise Larry would offer me some and I would have to think of an excuse to politely decline. Whatever he was eating smelled like rotten egg. If I didn't know any better, I would have thought he was chewing on a fart.

"Have you noticed that the days are all messed up?" he said as if reading my mind.

"Yeah," I replied.

"Maybe we should make our own days. I'm thinking every day can be called Fartday."

"Doesn't that defeat the purpose of naming the days of the week?"

Larry narrowed his eyes at me. "Fair enough. No naming the days then."

"Are you bored?" I asked, chuckling. "Because you only come up with this nonsense when you're bored or tired and you don't look tired."

Larry shrugged. "I may be a little bored. Also, these grapes Wallowbutt gave me tasted weird."

"Smells weird too," I added.

Larry frowned, then sniffed, then looked at the grape shaped thing in his hand again. "Is that where the smell is coming from? I thought someone farted and it was just lingering the entire time."

"Honestly, I wouldn't eat anything Wallowbutt gave me," I laughed.

"Wait," I heard a voice behind me. My blood chilled. It was Wallowbutt. "You didn't eat the smoke bombs I gave you, did you?"

Larry's eyes went wide and looked at the grapes that weren't actually grapes. "You said they were grapes!"

"Yes, I said they WERE grapes! Before I used them to make smoke bombs."

I cringed and turned to Wallowbutt, who, to my surprise, was holding back a laugh. "Why are you laughing? Isn't it dangerous?"

"Dangerous? Not at all. Tested it on myself. You can't trust weapons that look like food not to get eaten, you know? So I made it safe for ingestion." Wallowbutt pointed at Larry, who was now rubbing his tummy. I was able to hear it growling from almost all the way across the room. "Watch."

No sooner after he said it did Larry's eyes grow

wide and he let rip the most painful sounding fart I have ever heard. Green smoke filled the room and it smelled exactly like the stuff he had been eating. Only much, much worse. The smell took my breath away and I had to run from the room and the green fart cloud. Wallowbutt came running after me and when we were finally a safe distance away from Larry and his deadly butt, Wallowbutt shook his head.

"That's supposed to be used to escape. You throw it on the ground and a huge puff of fart smoke surrounds you. The smell confuses the zombies and it's thick enough so they can't see you running away. When the smoke finally clears up, you should be long gone. I gave it to Larry to try out on your mission but it seems he had other ideas." Wallowbutt tapped his index finger on his chin. "Then again, I probably should have told him it was a weapon and not delicious."

CHAPTER 6: SNOT ROCKET

The time finally came when we left the campus and headed into the wild. We were armed to the teeth with all kinds of fancy and weird weapons. Wallowbutt was truly an arms master and strapped so many grenades, rockets and blasters to us, we were hardly able to walk. Billy and Danny were excited to play with their new toys, but they didn't realize how big an issue being so over-encumbered actually was until we walked for about thirty minutes.

After we got sick of the complaining, Eve suggested that we dig a hole under a tree and bury the weapons we didn't need. We didn't even plan on getting into a fight at all. We didn't need any of these things.

And so, we dug a hole and got rid of most of our weapons, keeping only my and Larry's master blasters, a few fart grenades and smoke bombs, two snot rockets and a few ninja stars. The rest of the gang only kept the bare minimum as well. Madison, however, had her own arsenal strapped to her back that she refused to get rid of. I did not look forward to the complaining. If dad was correct, the airport was at least three hours from the campus. There was another two and a half hours left. A lot could happen in that time.

While we were walking, I took the time to examine the snot rockets. They were compatible with the master blasters and were an upgrade to the snot setting on the blaster. The rockets were shot into the air and covered everything below it in a layer of gross, green snot. I couldn't wait to use them.

When we reached the halfway mark at a little river, we decided that we were going to rest for a few minutes, have some snacks and then head out again. We wanted to be home by sundown and if we were going to make it, we had to hurry.

As if the zombies sensed that we were in a hurry, an entire horde emerged from the surrounding woods, desperate to slow us down. We were all on our feet instantly, waiting for them to make the first move. Us being this close to water was not a good thing at all. If we got rid of them this close to water, they were going to mutate and be an even bigger problem. Larry looked at me and as if we shared a mind, we nodded.

We had to distract them, slow them down. That way we could get away and when they finally had the ability to come after us again, we would be long gone.

Rocky growled at the approaching zombies, ready to attack as soon as I gave the order. No, we were not going to attack.

Larry tossed one of the smoke bombs into the horde of zombies, instantly creating a huge dome of smoke around them. If zombies could cough, I was sure they would have. The smell was just as bad as I remembered, but we didn't stick around too long to inhale much of it.

"Run," Larry yelled, and our entire group started sprinting.

Everyone except Madison.

"Michael!" I heard her yell and when I looked around, I saw that one of the zombies wasn't caught in the smoke and had a hold on Madison's ankle. Madison tried to pull away but couldn't reach her weapons.

Without thinking, I grabbed the snot rocket from my backpack and inserted it into my master blaster. Flipping the switch, I pulled the trigger and shot the rocket high into the air. It wasn't long until everyone, close to and in the smoke cloud was covered in snot, including Madison and the zombie.

I ran over to her and grabbed her hand, pulling her out of the sticky goop. She didn't say anything as she ran after the rest of the group. I didn't even get a thank you. Great… Now we were one snot rocket down and I didn't even get a thank you from my sister for saving her life. She really was the worst sister in the world. I should have left her for the zombie.

CHAPTER 7: NEVER A DULL

MOMENT

When we finally reached the airport, Madison was still trying to get snot out of her hair. I would have been lying if I said I didn't enjoy the sight. It was fun seeing her miserable. She has spent her life making me miserable and it was finally time for her to get some of her own medicine.

"Look at that!" Larry said as we crawled up a hill and reached the top. The hill overlooked the entire airport and it made spotting anything out of the ordinary very easy.

Once I was done laughing at my sister, I looked toward where Larry was pointing.

In the middle of the runway stood a giant UFO. It was round and had a million blinking lights on its body. It looked exactly like the ones I used to draw in school. You know? The ones that you saw on TV? If only I knew back then what I did now. I never would have drawn them. They were bad guys. Although, if you told me then that I was going to be a ninja, fighting the very aliens I was drawing, I would have laughed in your face.

"That thing is HUUUGE!" Danny said, his eyes growing bigger.

Billy elbowed him in the ribs. "Michael's parents said it was huge, didn't they? Don't act so surprised."

"Don't be mean," Eve said as she brought up the rear, a little out of breath. It was clear that she wasn't used to this much adventure. That was fine, she was going to get used to it soon enough if she stuck with us. "You two are always fighting and it's annoying. The enemy is over there." She pointed toward the airport.

"Agreed," Larry said. "And now we need a plan. Michael, Rocky and I will head to the ship and investigate. You guys stay here and keep a lookout."

"No way!" Madison said, gagging as she twisted her hair for the snot to drip out. "I did not get hit by a snot bomb just to stay out of the good part. I want to see what's in there as much as you guys."

"I'm also going," Eve said, glaring at Larry. "I've come this far."

"Us too," Billy and Danny agreed in unison. "No one is getting left behind. Besides, we're much safer if we stay in a group."

"I agree," I finally said. "We have to work together and stick together for that matter. We all go or none of us go."

Rocky barked in agreement. Larry sighed.

"Fine, but you have to be quiet. You have to do exactly what Michael and I do or they WILL hear us. And no one wants that. There has to be a hundred of them down there, not to mention the zombies surrounding the airport. We have to be very, very quiet. No one can hear a peep coming from us." Larry was obviously not very happy with everyone going, but there was no way that we were going to leave anyone behind. We were much safer together down there in the airport and out here with the zombies. If we stuck together, we had a fighting chance. If we stuck together, we could protect each other. Or at least try to.

CHAPTER 8: UFO'S AND DOG FARTS

It was surprisingly easy to reach the bottom of the hill and make our way to the airport. We were as silent as could be expected. Madison wasn't much of a problem. She was a ninja, after all.

She knew exactly how to be quiet. The rest of the group tiptoed and they really did their best, but they did step on leaves and branches every now and then which made me cringe. It was crazy how loud something so small could sound when you were trying to be quiet. Madison glared at Eve, Billy or Danny whenever they made a sound and I felt sorry for them. I have been on the end of that glare for a very, very long time and I can confirm that it has never been pleasant. It was a look that chilled my blood. Thank goodness I wasn't on the receiving end that day.

Rocky sniffed out the best route to the spaceship, his butt in the air and his nose on the ground. He let out a few small farts as he went. It was probably the weird situation that was making him gassy. The smell was horrible and it was a mission in itself to keep from gagging and making more noise than anyone else. That surely would have gotten me a Madison glare.

There were aliens all over the place in the airport. Some had orange skin, others had purple, others had blue. They were a rainbow of aliens and I would have thought it was cool were they not trying to take over our planet. That wasn't very cool at all. Not one bit.

When we reached an open gap in the fence, Larry climbed through and told us to wait. He made his way toward the spaceship, as silent as a mouse. Whenever an alien looked his way, Larry slipped behind something, hidden completely from view. I could only wish to be as good a shinobi as he was someday. He was truly something I aspired to be. Larry reached the spacecraft and made his way up the lowered ramp. He was checking if everything was clear before he popped his head out and waved us over. The coast was clear and we were able to make it into the spaceship without much trouble.

"Where do we go now?" I whispered, looking at the long hallway of doors that stretched out in front of us. The spaceship looked even bigger on the inside than it did from the outside. There must have been hundreds of doors on each side. Who knew where those doors led? I wished we had time to explore the ship, but we didn't and we had to find any form of clue to what they were carrying and how many more of these ships were coming as soon as we could. The plan was to get in and get out as quickly as humanly possible.

"I don't know," Larry said, looking at the gang, then at me, then at Rocky. He narrowed his eyes at Rocky. "Hey," Larry bent down to whisper to my dog. "Can you sniff out where we need to go? We need to find something useful.

Rocky nodded, and pressed his nose to the floor again. I instantly pinched my nose, knowing

42

what we were going to have to follow all the way through the spaceship. I was not looking forward to it. Although, I had to admit that Rocky's farts were what legends were made of.

CHAPTER 9: SWITCHES AND ACCIDENTS

The inside of the spaceship had more lights than the entire town combined. There were flickering lights among the constant glowing ones. Those beeped every time the light went out.

The metal inside of the ship glowed a green and purple, giving it a creepy feel. I could tell that the rest of the gang felt the same way as they were walking close behind Larry and me. Rocky led the way, his nose pressed to the floor of the ship. He knew what we were looking for even if we didn't. We only came here to check things out after all, not to actually find anything. But Rocky knew something we didn't, and we had to trust him. He was a special dog, after all. If he could throw ninja stars, he could know things that we didn't too. We had to trust him.

We followed Rocky to a weird looking room filled with buttons, levers and wheels. I didn't even want to know what all of those things did. I could only imagine what horrors could be unleashed on the Earth if we were to press one of the buttons accidentally. I didn't think any of us would be able to live with ourselves if we did.

Rocky ran straight toward a large, red button in the middle of the room. Eve was the first one to step up and investigate.

"What is it, boy?" she asked as she examined the button from all angles. Eve leaned down to read the warning on a label underneath the button. "Do not touch. Horrible things will follow."

I shivered. "What kind of horrible things do you

think it means?"

"Do you think it'll call down more ships?" Danny asked with big eyes.

Then Billy spoke. "What if it turns the zombies into clowns? I hate clowns. Please don't let them turn the zombies into clowns."

"There aren't any clowns," Madison grumbled. "Grow up. Nothing can be worse than what's already here, right? We might as well press it and find out." She walked forward, fully intent on pressing the button. It was Larry who stopped her from doing something stupid.

"Don't touch that!" he said. He seemed angry. I have never seen Larry anything but cool. "We already have our hands full with the zombies. Do you really want to make it worse for us? That would not be a very shinobi thing to do. Do you really want to betray us like this?"

Madison crossed her arms and looked at the floor. "No, sir."

Before Larry could say anything else, I saw movement in the corner of my eye. When I turned to see what it was, I saw one of the aliens staring at us. It was obvious that he didn't expect to see us.

Eve let out a small yelp and then chaos followed.

Eve must have taken a step back and accidentally pressed the button with her hip because the whole room lit up and a siren went off. The alien looked at the blinking lights, then at us, then at Eve next to the button, who now had covered her mouth with one hand.

"What have you done?" The alien said. He was one of the ones with orange skin. It looked as if he had glitter on his skin whenever the blinking light hit him. "You have ruined everything!"

"Ruined it?" I said, frowning. "How did we ruin it? That was one of your weapons."

"That button makes it so that no zombie can infect another human being. No scratches, no bites. The button was there for an emergency if the zombies ever decided to turn on us! Now you have ruined the entire plan." The alien's nose holes flared. If his voice didn't say he was angry, his expression sure did. If he had eyebrows, it would have been horrifying.

We all looked at each other, not knowing whether we should be celebrating or not. No more infections! The zombies were still there and hungry for brains, but this was a start. This was a very good start.

"You will not get away with this!" the alien promised and turned to run away. He was going to alert the guards! He was going to tell all of them that we were there.

"We can't let him get away," I said, and Rocky took that as a direct order. Rocky barked as he ran after the alien, not caring if we followed or not.

CHAPTER 10: CATCHING UP

It took us a while to catch up to the alien. Even with Rocky's ninja speed, he struggled to keep up with him. Only when the alien came to a stop did we catch up. And boy, did I wish we hadn't.

Waiting for us at the bottom of the ramp we used

to get into the spaceship was an entire army of aliens! We stopped in our tracks when we saw them, taking a single step back.

I recognized one of them as the one that had stopped us outside of the bunker. He looked at us and grinned as he stepped forward.

"I see that you have saved us the trouble of coming to get you. Now you have delivered yourself to our doorstep," he said in his robotic voice. The orange one that we were chasing whispered something in his ear and his nostrils flared. I took a step back, small, silent farts escaping from all directions. I think even Madison let a few rip. It was the sort of fart that you only got when you were nervous. The fart that made your stomach ache until you let it go.

Rocky got into position to fight, ready for my command. Larry stepped forward, taking his place as the leader of our little group.

"You have foiled our plans!" The alien said, his voice rising. "Without the zombies being able to create more zombies, the human race has a chance of survival. How dare you?"

Larry shrugged, then looked back to wink at me. He had this in the bag. The wink told me that. The wink also told me that we had to be ready to run when he gave the order. We were all ready.

"I don't know who gave you the right to be angry at us for defending our planet, Mr. Alien. But I can assure you that we will not stop until our planet is our own again."

The alien laughed, and soon a choir of laughter came from his army. "I'd like to see that happen," he said with a scary smile on his face. He had something up his sleeve, I could feel it. "I don't think that will happen though, seeing as your president is already on a ship sent into space. I don't think anyone can fight back when their leader isn't even on their planet."

I looked at the team and they looked at me, horrified. The aliens have kidnapped the president? How did they even manage that? How did they get past the guards? The president was supposed to be the most protected person in the world. Then again, if they were able to take over an entire planet, maybe they could easily abduct the president.

"We don't need the zombies to take over the planet. We just need to break the spirit of its inhabitants." The alien seemed way too smug for my liking.

"That's not going to be nearly as easy as you think it is," Larry said with an arrogant shrug. "It's not going to be easy with ninja's defending the Earth. We have weapons, we have a team that we can trust and we have skill. What do you have? None of that. You rely on us to destroy ourselves. You are not a villain. You are a weakling and we will get our planet back."

Larry's words seemed to trigger the alien. "Let's see how arrogant you are when my people take care of you. The zombies might not be able to turn you, but our serums can. We made backups."

And then the alien smiled before his army stormed toward us.

CHAPTER 11: UNLIKELY HERO

What followed was a battle of epic proportions. Honestly, it was something out of a superhero movie. Only, this wasn't a movie and we were the superheroes.

The army ran at us and my first instinct was to

run back up the ramp of the ship and try to close it somehow. That wasn't what happened though. Larry instructed Billy, Danny and Eve to get on the ship and figure out a way to lift the ramp. It was our job, the team of ninjas, to hold off the aliens as long as possible to buy them some time. I didn't know what we were gonna do when we got in the spacecraft. Surely we couldn't stay in there forever. But that was a problem we had to sort out later. The problem at hand was much bigger.

Madison took out her own mini blaster that looked almost identical to the master blasters Larry and I had. Only hers was in the shape of a pistol. She flipped a switch and shot the alien closest to her, enveloping him in a bubble that floated up, up, up… For a moment I looked at the alien as he gasped for breath, clawing at the confines of the bubble.

"Fart bubble," she said casually with a shrug.

I cringed. Being trapped in a bubble made of farts? Well, that just sounded brutal, even for these aliens.

Larry pulled out his master blaster and so did I. We shot at the aliens, pushing them back. We gave them everything we had but nothing seemed to keep them away for long enough.

Rocky was right in the middle of the fight, knocking aliens off their feet by swiping his hind legs across the ground, or using his front paws to whack them behind the head, knocking them out entirely. I tossed some ninja stars his way and he kicked them expertly with his paws, directing them toward the incoming horde of aliens. The stars landed in their guns and utility belts. This caused the guns to seize and their utility belts that held the rest of their weapons to fall to the floor. Still, this made little to no difference. There were too many of them and our time was running out.

"How far is the ramp?" I asked in a panic, eyeing the horde.

"Give us a few more minutes!" Eve shouted. I could hear her pressing button after button, desperate to find the one that controlled the ramp.

Lifting my master blaster, I switched to the snot setting and aimed at the alien closest to me. He was stuck in place instantly and it didn't seem like he had any way of getting out. Grinning at each other, Madison, Larry and I each switched to the snot setting of our blasters and shot away. Whenever Madison's snot was on cool down, she switched to her fart bubble gun. Soon enough there were tons of aliens in the sky, choking and gagging on the smell in the bubble. On the ground, they were stuck, rooted in place by the snot. For how long, I didn't know. All I knew was that Eve had to hurry or we were going to be in tons of trouble.

"We got it!" Danny yelled, and on cue, the ramp of the spacecraft started pulling up. "Get in!"

In unison, the three of us turned back and ran toward the spaceship's gaping entrance that was now slowly closing. We were probably gonna have to jump to reach the entrance. Rocky was trailing behind us, growling and snapping toward anyone who came too close to us. He had our backs just like I knew he would. He was the best dog in the world.

Larry grabbed Madison and lifted her into the ship, then he did the same for me followed by Rocky. I was so relieved that I let go of a small fart that squeaked and made everyone inside the spaceship giggle. We giggled until we realized that Larry wasn't going to make it. One of the aliens held on to him tightly, making sure that he couldn't get to us. The entrance was getting smaller and smaller and I panicked.

Madison surprised us all when she grabbed the snot rocket from my belt and attached it to her pistol. Before I could warm her of the recoil, she shot the rocket into the horde of aliens, trapping them firmly in place. I wanted to tell her that she was being stupid. That she had trapped Larry down

there too, but then she switched to the fart bubbled
and shot one right at Larry. At first I wanted to yell
at her, to ask her what she was doing, but then I
saw that the bubble was pulling Larry away from
the Alien that had his grip on my best friend. The
bubbled floated him up, and Larry pinched his
nose, holding his breath.

Madison looked around the entrance of the ship
frantically until she found a rope. She grabbed it
and quickly tied a loop. I wouldn't have believed

the next part if I didn't see it for my own eyes. Madison swirled the loop over her head, and then cowboy style, managed to toss the loop over Larry and tighten it around his waist. The bubble popped but Madison was already pulling him toward us. Larry rolled into the spaceship right before the ramp closed and the shouting from the aliens became a low hum. Larry was covered in snot, but I didn't care. I ran toward him and hugged him tightly. I thought I had lost him. I thought I would never see him again.

Larry chuckled and hugged me back, wiping snot all over my back. It was gross but it was so worth it.

"Madison, you were awesome!" Billy said in awe and I turned around to look at my sister. She actually was awesome. I would have just stayed there and watched as the aliens took my fart brother. Madison was amazing.

Without thinking about it, I wrapped my arms around my sister, hugging her tightly. To my surprise, she didn't push me away. Instead she hugged me back. "Thank you," was all I could say.

"You guys would do the same for me," she said, and then pushed me away. Madison looked at the snot print I'd left on her and she cringed. "Aw, man! I just got all of it off me!"

I burst out laughing, shaking my head. Poor Madison was covered in snot all over again.

CHAPTER 12: COME IN, THIS IS

THE WHITE HOUSE

"Now what?" Madison asked as she picked snot out of her hair. The rest of us just looked at each other. We had no idea what we had to do now either.

I shrugged. "I guess we have a look around on the ship and see if we can find anything useful. Perhaps we can find some weapons that can destroy the aliens. I don't know. We can't just sit here doing nothing."

"I agree," said Eve. "Just sitting around and waiting for someone to rescue us is not going to help us in any way, shape or form."

Larry nodded. "We might as well. We stick together," he said and everyone nodded in agreement. "Keep your eyes and your ears open. There might still be a straggler alien in the ship. We need to be on our guard and ready for anything. The battle isn't over yet."

With that, we walked down the hall, the lights giving it an eerie feel. When we reached the first door, we shared a look. I think we were all a bit scared to open it, not knowing what waited for us on the other side. That was the scariest part of all. What if we had just gotten away from the aliens outside and opened a door to a room full of new ones? If they attacked us, we were trapped in here with them and there was no way to get away.

I looked at Rocky. "Can you smell if there is anyone else on the other side of this door?" I whispered and he nodded. I have gotten so used to Rocky nodding, I didn't even notice that it was strange for a dog to do stuff like that.

Rocky pressed his snout to the crack at the bottom of the door. Giving a few sniffs. When he came back up, he shook his head. There was no one inside.

Regardless of what Rocky said, Larry, Madison and I still held our guns high as Billy reached for the button on the side of the door to open it. The door slid open with a satisfying woosh and revealed an empty room. No, not an empty room. This looked like an empty apartment. There was a kitchen in it, a living room with a big television, and a door that most probably led to a bedroom. The team shared a look. My parents were right. They were transporting people. If the other rooms looked like this one, there was no doubt about it.

In silence, we moved on to the next door where Rocky repeated his process of expertly sniffing the room behind the door. It must have been terrible to be a dog in a zombie apocalypse, I realized. With their sense of smell, it was truly a punishment. If the smell was bad for us, I didn't want to know what it was like for Rocky.

The exact same room was behind this door too. I frowned, walked back to the previous room and checked that we weren't looking at the same room again. It was strange, the rooms looked exactly

62

alike. Even the decorations were exactly in the same spot even though they were completely different rooms. I wondered for a moment how boring life on Earth would have been if every house was the same and no one was permitted to be different. At that moment I was proud of how unique our planet was and it horrified me to think that the aliens wanted to turn Earth into this monstrosity. That was even scarier than the aliens and the zombies combined. Them turning our Earth into something it's not, into something that took away our uniqueness made me angry. I shook the thought out of my head. That wasn't going to happen. We were going to find a way out of this mess one way or another. I wouldn't rest until we did. We were not going down without a fight, not if we had a say in it.

Room after room, we repeated the process and every time, we found another, boring room just like the previous one.

It was only when we reached the middle of the hall when we found something different. The room seemed to be in the dead center of the spaceship and above us was a glass panel. Through the panel we could see the sky beyond and the sunset that was drawing nearer and nearer. We had to get home. The only problem was that I had no idea how we were going to do that. How were we going to get home when there was an entire army of aliens outside the spaceship?

"Come in, come in, this is the White House," a voice said, and we all looked at each other, expecting one of us to have pulled a prank. None of us seemed to know where the voice was coming from. Again, the mysterious voice spoke. "Come in, come in, this is the White House. Can anyone hear us?"

Rocky followed the noise and barked as he came to the source. Everyone rushed over to see. The voice was coming from speakers that had more buttons than a telephone. Larry shrugged and pushed a random button.

"This is Larry. We can hear you, White House."

"Larry," The voice on the other end of the line sounded relieved. "We need your help. I'm afraid without you, all is lost."

CHAPTER 13: SPACE HEROES

Were we really talking to the people in the White House? Did they really need our help? Rocky was shifting on his feet in excitement and I could have sworn there was a pungent fart smell in the air from someone's silent-but-deadly butt. I couldn't say for sure, though. No one looked particularly guilty. It might even have been me. I wouldn't have put it past me. I was so anxious, it could have been one of those farts that escaped without you knowing it.

"Who are you and how did you get on this radio?" the voice from the speaker asked.

Larry pressed the button again to answer. "I am only a janitor but I am here with some very heroic kids. We are trapped in an alien spacecraft after we were attacked. The aliens are locked out but in turn, we are locked in. We managed to stop the zombies from infecting more people. That threat should be a little less now."

"The zombies can no longer infect survivors? What about a cure? Have you found that?"

Larry frowned. "No cure yet. We were looking into the giant spaceship at the airport when we found the control room. No cure, only a way for it to be managed until we actually do find a cure."

The voice sighed. "I suppose that is better than nothing. You are truly a hero. I don't know how the radio frequency got to the spaceship. They must have hacked into the radios. That works out perfectly for us, though. The president needs help and you are the only ones on a vessel that can carry you into space to get him. You are the only people we were able to contact since the president was taken. He might have a cure and we need his guidance. You have to go into space and find him. You have to bring him back to Earth."

"We can't drive a spaceship," I whispered to Larry.

"Relax! It's just like driving a car." Larry paused for a moment. "I think."

"Space is a big place," Larry said as he pushed the button again. "How are we going to find the president?"

"The president has a tracking device in his suit. I will send you the coordinates. But enough talking. Talk it over with your team. By the sound of things, you don't have any other way out of there other than going up. Why not save the world while you are escaping?"

Everyone looked at each other. Larry was the first one to speak. "I think we should do it."

"It's risky to say the least," Eve interjected, looking at the speaker, then toward the closed ramp. We could just slightly hear a banging on it. The aliens were trying to get in. "But if we stay here, they will get us."

Billy nodded. "Besides, can you just imagine what it will be like to save the president? We'll be heroes!"

Danny high-fived Billy. "Dude! Imagine what we can buy with all the reward money."

"Heroes aren't heroes for the reward," Madison shrugged. "Heroes are heroes because it's the right thing to do. I say we do it."

I was shocked at how selfless Madison sounded. Then again, she did save Larry from a horde of angry aliens. Maybe I have misjudged her all of these years. Maybe she wasn't so bad after all.

"I agree with my sister. We are ninjas and we have vowed to protect the world from evil. With you guys helping us," I turned to Eve, Billy and Danny. "We might just be able to pull this thing off."

Larry grinned when he pushed the button again. "Count us in. The next time you hear from us, we will have the president on board."

"You are heroes," the voice from the other side of the speaker said. "This will not be forgotten. Suit up. You have a long journey ahead of you."

With that, the voice disappeared and the seven of us, including Rocky, were staring at each other. We were actually going to be national heroes! If the president really did have the cure, it was going to save the entire world.

"Well, kids, you heard the woman. Suit up!" Everyone grinned excitedly and went to look for space suits. Everyone except Larry, Rocky and me. Larry nudged me with an elbow. "Looks like you can add astronaut to your resume, little dude. And this here doggo is going to become the first-ever space ninja dog!" Rocky barked excitedly.

I was about to say something when an awful smell lined my nostrils. "What is that smell?!"

One look at Larry's smug grin told me that it was him. That fiend!

I choked on the smell as we burst out laughing. "That hit me from every single angle, man!"

And then, when the smell was finally blowing over and we stopped laughing, I looked at my fart brother and my ninja dog, and grinned.

Simultaneously, all three of us lifted our left legs, and let out a choir of farts. We were going to save the world, one fart at a time.

ALMOST LIFTOFF

We are about to lift off and take on a new
adventure in space. I hope that my family is alright
but I keep on telling myself that the campus was
safe, Wallowbutt was with them, and my parents
were ninjas just like me. They could take care of
themselves perfectly fine.

I am excited about what is to come, but I am also a little nervous. I have never even been on a plane before, never mind a spaceship. Larry says he can fly this thing, but I am not so sure after I have witnessed his bus driving skills firsthand.

Rocky is excited and the White House has sent us some very special training exercises to get Rocky started for space. Apparently, dogs can be very useful in space if they are trained right.

Madison is back to her awful self, but that's okay, I can live with it. She saved my fart brother and that was all that mattered. I am willing to forget the bad stuff she says and does sometimes. I know that on the inside, she isn't as bad as I always thought. Just don't tell her that, though! I wouldn't want her to think that I actually like her.

I also discovered something else today.

As funny as farts are, they are not very funny when you are wearing a spacesuit and only you can smell your own gas. I had to learn that the hard way. Billy has snot stuck on the inside of his helmet but can't wipe it away while he is wearing the suit. I suppose he just has to try and look around it. That was a sneeze he is never going to forget.

All in all, I am excited for the adventure that is to come, and I know that with my friends and my dog, we can do this. We are going to save the president as well as save the world. We are heroes.

No, we are ninjas.

And who knows, Maybe our friends will be able to prove themselves and become ninjas too. Who knows what the future holds for us?

ABOUT THE AUTHOR

C A TREANOR & I DOSANJH

Caroline Treanor is a children's author with an imaginative, rhythmic writing style writing for little children and a funny and inspirational style when writing for older kids. The combination of catchy rhymes and humorous imagination along with positive thinking messages appeals to the hearts of children.

Writing with her own childrens' help and creative minds, her goal is to create children's books that are engaging, funny, and inspirational for kids of all ages. The adults will enjoy them too as much as

she has enjoyed creating them.

She has recently begun translating her work into several languages, including Spanish and Japanese to reach and delight new audiences around the

World.

Caroline and her three children live in the UK with their two black cats, Layla and Bella who feature in the 'Clever Baby Series' early learning books.

We hope you have an enjoyable reading experience!

DIARY OF A NINJA KID 1:

CLOUDY WITH A CHANCE OF

ZOMBIES

Blurb:

My name is Michael carter, and I am a Ninja Kid!!

I wasn't always one!! A zombie apocalypse. Are you ready for one?

Michael Carter is 12 years old. Everything is going wrong in his life. Every. Single. Thing.

New house. New school. A sister that went to a torture academy. Parents that love him but are just too busy to see.

The only good thing is Rocky, his dog. Until he learns about the ninja code. But, can a code help against the danger he is suddenly faced with? Does he or Rocky even stand a chance?

Are you willing to wade through an apocalypse of zombie farts to find out?

Read these pages if you dare. But hold your nose if you do!

Ready to laugh your socks off?

WARNING: THIS BOOK CONTAINS FARTS!

DIARY OF A NINJA KID 2:

STORMY WITH A TON OF

ZOMBIES!

Blurb:

Michael Carter is ready for whatever the world wants to throw his way. He is a ninja, after all! Nothing can stand in his way.

With a handful of new friends, a dog with secret abilities and his fart brother, Michael has to find a safe place for them to settle.

But when he finds some secrets about his family and the cause of the zombie invasion, Michael has to try and cope with everything going on. The zombie apocalypse was caused by aliens who want to take over earth.

For what reason, and will Michael ever find out? Will he and his new friends have to live in hiding for the rest of their lives, or will Wallowbutt's fart grenades be enough to save them all?

AUTHOR NOTE:

We would like to thank you, our readers, for joining us on Michael, Larry and Rocky's adventure!

There are many more great adventures in store for us in **Diary Of A Ninja Kid 4: Silent But Violent**, the scary adventures of the ghost pirates!

For the opportunity to receive lots of exciting extras and to keep up to date with our next books, please **subscribe to our mailing list** through our website, carolinetreanorintbooks.com/subscribe, and like our **Facebook** page, @CATPublishingInternational.

ABOUT THE ILLUSTRATORS

COVER DESIGN BY BEX SUTTON

Bex Sutton is the founder of Primal Studios, an Illustration, Graphic Design & Marketing Studio based in Plymouth, UK. As the Head Designer, she works on a variety of projects, from children's book illustrations to t-shirt designs.

With the company of her husband, two cats and

giant puppy, she can be found drawing day and night on her computer, losing herself in a new magical world she designs.

Experienced with working with large companies such as Scrabble and PartyCasino, and small, independent clients and companies, she has a wealth of experience in the design industry.

With her illustrations and art direction helping indie author's hit #1 in the Amazon.com's New Release lists, coupled with an impressive portfolio that shows a range of styles and skills, she is a professional but friendly person to add to your design team!

She can be reached by email at bex@primalst.com

INTERNAL DESIGNS BY NAZIFA TASNIM

Nazifa Tasnim is a childrens' book Illustrator. She focuses on many different storylines , fictional characters as well as mysterious creatures and environments which help her style and talent to be unique and imaginative for her audience. She is also fascinated by abstract and realistic artworks and has a varied set of artistic illustration skills.

Ingram Content Group UK Ltd.
Milton Keynes UK
UKHW050801070323
418120UK00001B/23